MAGIC BONE

ROOTIN' TOOTIN' COW DOG

GROSSET & DUNLAP
Penguin Young Readers Group
An Imprint of Penguin Random House LLC

Text copyright © 2015 by Nancy Krulik. Illustrations copyright © 2015
by Sebastien Braun. All rights reserved. Published by Grosset & Dunlap,
an imprint of Penguin Random House LLC, 345 Hudson Street,
New York, New York 10014. GROSSET & DUNLAP is a trademark
of Penguin Random House LLC. Manufactured in China.

Library of Congress Control Number: 2014041559

Part of Boxed Set ISBN 9781101950654   10 9 8 7 6 5 4 3 2 1

MAGIC
BONE

ROOTIN' TOOTIN'
COW DOG

by Nancy Krulik
illustrated by Sebastien Braun

Grosset & Dunlap
An Imprint of Penguin Random House

For Josie B., who inspires me endlessly—NK

To Mallory—thanks for your guidance!—SB

CHAPTER 1

"Get off me!" Samson grumbles angrily. "It's not my job to give rides!"

Samson is the old mixed-breed who lives next door to me. I've never heard him so upset. I wonder what's going on.

I hurry over to my fence and peek at him through the holes. Samson's two-leg is sitting in a chair. There's a mini two-leg sitting on Samson's back.

The mini two-leg is smiling, which

is something both two-legs and dogs do when they are happy.

But Samson isn't smiling. And he isn't happy.

"I said, get off!" Samson barks. He kicks his back legs in the air.

Wham! The mini two-leg falls off his back.

Whaaa! The mini two-leg's not smiling anymore. She's screaming. *Whaaa!*

Samson's two-leg starts shouting, too. I don't understand a lot of two-leg words. But I do understand "bad dog." And I know that means Samson is in trouble.

Samson's two-leg carries the mini two-leg into the house and closes the door, leaving Samson outside alone.

"I can't believe my two-leg yelled at me," Samson grumbles.

"Two-legs do that a lot," says Frankie, the German shepherd who lives on the other side of my house.

I guess Frankie was watching from behind his fence, too.

"Ever since that mini two-leg came to visit, she's been crawling on my back," Samson explains. "It was making me nuts. So I threw her off."

"Makes sense to me," Frankie says.

"It's not my job to carry a little two-leg around," Samson continues. "I'm a dog, not a horse."

"Right," I say. "I've never met a dog who had a job giving rides to two-legs."

Frankie laughs. "It's not like you've met that many dogs, Sparky," he says. "You only hang out with Samson and me."

Frankie always thinks he knows everything. But I know something he *doesn't* know: I have met lots of dogs.

4

And I can meet new dogs any time I want. All I need is my magic bone. The one I have buried under the flowers in my yard.

My magic bone is a secret. No one knows about it. Not Frankie or Samson or even my two-leg, Josh. Of course, I couldn't tell Josh about the magic bone, even if I wanted to. I don't speak two-leg. And Josh doesn't speak dog.

My magic bone is amazing. One big bite and *kaboom*! I go far, far away. One time my magic bone *kaboomed* me all the way to Tokyo, Japan. I got to eat squishy fishy called sashimi with some Ninja Dogs. They had a cool job—protecting the statue of a famous Japanese Akita named Hachikō.

And then there was the time my bone *kaboomed* me all the way to Zermatt, Switzerland. I met a Saint Bernard there named Lena. I helped her save some two-legs who were stuck on a mountain during a snowstorm. Now Lena saves two-legs all the time. That's a really important job.

The Ninja Dogs and Lena work really hard. But I never

see Frankie or Samson working.

"Do you have a job?" I ask Samson.

Samson thinks for a minute. "Well, I guess it's my job to get my two-leg his slippers," he says.

"What are slippers?" I ask him.

"The things two-legs put over their paws when they walk around the house," Samson explains.

"Josh just walks around in his bare paws in our house," I tell Samson.

"Lucky you," Frankie tells me.

"That's one less job you have to do. I have two jobs. I have to get my two-leg his slippers *and* his newspaper."

"What is a newspaper?" I ask Frankie.

"It's a bunch of rolled-up paper that's always on our grass in the morning," Frankie tells me. "It's my job to fetch it and bring it inside. I don't know why my two-leg makes me do that, because he always gets mad when I bring it back with tooth marks or spit on it."

"That's not your fault," I tell Frankie. "Mouths have teeth and spit."

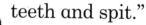

"I know," Frankie says. "If he doesn't want bite marks and spit on his newspaper, he shouldn't make me fetch it."

Frankie and Samson sound angry with their two-legs. But I am never angry with mine. Josh is the best. He plays fetch with me. He feeds me. And he knows exactly where to *scratchity, scratch, scratch* when I'm itchy.

Samson lets out a yawn. "All this talk about working is making me tired. I think I'll take a nap in the sun."

"Sounds great to me," Frankie agrees.

"Me too," I say.

"What are you tired from?" Frankie asks me. "You don't have a job. You're just a puppy."

"Enjoy it while you can," Samson tells me. "When you grow up, your two-leg will expect you to do jobs for him."

"And if you don't, he might get a dog who will instead," Frankie adds.

"Leave the puppy alone," Samson tells Frankie. "You're scaring him."

I'll say. I don't want Josh to get another dog.

I lie down on the cool, wet grass and close my eyes.

But I can't sleep. I keep thinking about what Frankie said.

I don't want Josh to get a new dog. I have to learn a job. But what can I do?

Josh doesn't wear slippers.

There's never a paper on our lawn.

Josh doesn't get lost in the snow.

And he doesn't have a statue I can guard.

I can't *thinkety, think, think* of a thing that I can do around here.

I don't want to think anymore. I want to play. Or better yet . . . I want to *dig*.

That's my favorite thing to do!

I race over to Josh's flower bed.

Diggety, dig, dig. Dirt flies everywhere. I'm digging a deep, deep hole. *Diggety, dig . . .*

There it is! My bone. My bright, beautiful, sparkly magic bone. Sitting right in the middle of my hole.

Sniffety, sniff, sniff. My bone smells good. Like chicken, beef, and sausage all rolled into one.

I just *have* to take a bite . . . *CHOMP*!

Wiggle, waggle, whew. I feel dizzy—like my insides are spinning all around—but my outsides are standing still. Stars are twinkling in front of my eyes—even though it's daytime! All around me I smell food—fried chicken, salmon, roast beef. But there isn't any food in sight.

Kaboom! Kaboom! Kaboom!

CHAPTER 2

Owie, ow, ow! Something just stung my butt.

The *kabooming* has stopped. I'm definitely not in my yard anymore. My yard has soft grass. But the only thing under my paws here is dry, rocky dirt.

It was warm in my yard. But here it's really hot.

There aren't any stinger-thingers in my yard. But here . . . *Owie, ow, ow!*

I turn around. There's a strange

bush behind me. It doesn't have soft green leaves like the bushes in my yard. Its leaves are sharp. And they hurt when you back into them. I'm not sure I'm going to like this place.

I have to bury my bone to keep it safe while I go exploring. I don't want some other dog stealing my bone. I'm going to need it when it's time for me to go home.

So I start digging. *Diggety, dig, dig.* Dry dirt and little rocks fly all over the place. My hole is getting bigger and bigger. And deeper and deeper. I wonder if hole digging could be a job.

Probably not. Sometimes Josh gets mad when I dig too many holes in our yard.

But there's no one here to get mad. So I *diggety, dig, dig* some more. Then I drop my bone into the hole and push the dirt back over it.

A warm wind blows. I smell food! Meaty *two-leg* food. *Yummy, yum, yum!* I'd sure like some!

Sniffety, sniff, sniff. I'm following my nose. My nose is smart. It knows where to find meat.

Come on, paws. Walk faster. I'm hungry!

There are two-legs to the right of me. And there are two-legs to the left of me.

There are two-legs all around me!

I don't know where I am. But I know it's crowded. There are four-legs here, too. I can smell them. And I can see their paw prints in the dirt.

But I'm not interested in *any* legs right now. I'm interested in food. And I smell plenty of that! But I'll never get to it. Not with all these two-legs blocking my path.

"Move, two-legs!" I bark.

Wiggle, waggle, wow! These two-legs must speak dog. Because they all begin to move away from me. Some go to the right. Some go to the left.

They've left me a clear path to the food. "Thank you, two-legs!" I bark.

NEIGH!

I turn around and see a white horse. He has a two-leg on his back. Right. Like Samson said, giving rides to two-legs is a horse's job.

NEIGH!   NEIGH!   NEIGH! NEIGH! NEIGH!

Uh-oh! Now there's not just one horse. There are five of them. They're all running this way, side by side, and taking up the whole path.

NEIGH! NEIGH!

Cling clang!

Boom. Boom.

Uh-oh! Now it's not just horses coming up behind me. There's also a huge red metal machine with big round paws.

And a group of two-legs banging on things that make loud noises.

They're coming fast. And it doesn't look like they're stopping!

"Get out of the way! The Grand Entrance Parade is coming your way!"

Suddenly I hear a dog. I look around to see a Blue Lacy calling to

me. He's between a bunch of two-leg legs.

"You'd better move it! Those horses will trample you!" he yells.

He's right. I have to get out of the way. But there's nowhere to go. Two-legs are standing on both sides of the path. They are all squeezed together. They haven't left any room for me.

"Come on!" he shouts. "I'll make room."

The Blue Lacy is crazy. There's no room for me in that crowd.

Suddenly, the Blue Lacy picks up his leg and lets out a big stream of yellow water. The two-legs standing around him push and shove at one another to get out of the way.

Now there's a big space for me to stand.

"Thanks," I say as I race over to him.

"What were you thinking?" the Blue Lacy asks me. "Why would you walk right in the path of the parade that opens the rodeo?"

"Opens the what-ee-o?" I have no idea what he's talking about.

The Blue Lacy cocks his head. "You mean you've never been to a rodeo?"

I shake my head.

"Yeehaw! Your first rodeo," he says. "Welcome, pardner!"

"My name's not Pardner," I tell him. "It's Sparky."

The Blue Lacy laughs at that. "Howdy, Sparky," he says. "I'm Rex."

"Hi, Rex," I say.

"Welcome to the rodeo, Sparky," Rex says. "The greatest place on earth!"

"Can't be," I tell him.

"Why not?" Rex asks.

"Josh's house is the greatest place

on earth," I explain. "Because that's where Josh is."

"Does Josh's house have events like cow roping and bull riding?" Rex asks.

I shake my head. I don't think so. I don't even know what those are.

"Does Josh's house have a midway where you can find food, rides, and games?" Rex asks.

"We have food," I say.

"Not like rodeo food," Rex insists. "There's nothing like Texas barbecue."

Rex sure talks strange. "What-zas what-ee-cue?" I ask him.

Rex gives me a funny look. "Texas," he says. "The Lone Star State?"

I shake my head. I really don't know what he's talking about.

"I'm not sure where you're from,"

Rex says, "but you're in Texas now. And barbecue is this meat that's cooked . . . well . . . I can't describe it. You just have to taste it."

Taste. Now *that's* something I understand.

"I'd love to," I tell Rex.

"Okay, pardner," Rex says. "Follow me over yonder to the midway!"

I think about telling Rex my name is Sparky, again. And I think about asking him what a midway is. But I figure it's probably better to just follow him. Because Rex is going where the food is, and that's exactly where I want to be.

CHAPTER 3

"*Yummy, yum, yum!*" I exclaim a few minutes later as I swallow some sweet blue sticky stuff I found on the ground. The food that's on the ground is for dogs. That's the rule in my house. I guess it's the rule here, too, because Rex just gobbled up some of the sticky stuff.

"Cotton candy is delicious," Rex says. "Two-legs are really sloppy eaters. Which means more for us."

I see something bright red on the ground. It looks really good. So I grab it with my mouth. *Yummy, yum, yum!*

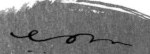

This is sweet and sticky. My tail likes it, too. It starts wagging all around. Which is strange, since my tail doesn't have a mouth. It can't taste anything.

"You like that candy apple, huh?" Rex asks me.

"Iff defishes . . ." I'm trying to say *it's delicious*, but my teeth are stuck together. I wiggle my snout, trying to unstick myself.

Rex laughs and reaches his nose up in the air. "I smell barbecue with all the fixin's," he tells me. "Let's go get some!"

I follow Rex through the crowd of two-legs. A meaty bone! *CHOMP!* I take

a big bite. Soft, chewy meat falls off
the bone and fills my mouth. Sweet,
sticky sauce slides down my throat.

"This is amazing," I say.

"Rootin' tootin' right," Rex says.
"Texas barbecue is the best barbecue
there is!"

I look down at the ground, hoping
to find another bone. There isn't
one. But there is something else that
looks tasty. It's bright red. Just like
that *yummy, yum, yum* candy apple.

I open my mouth . . .

"Sparky," Rex shouts. "Don't eat the chili . . ."
CHOMP!
". . . pepper!"

"Owie, ow, ow!" I don't know what this is. But it's not a candy apple. It's not sweet at all. It's hot and spicy. *Really* hot and spicy. My mouth is burning.

I need water. Lots and lots of water.

I spot a group of two-legs standing around a big water bowl. One of the two-legs is filling small bowls with water from the big one.

I need that water. And I need it *now*.

My paws run to the big water bowl. Fast. Faster. *Fastest!*

My paws are running so fast my fur flies in my eyes. I can't see where I'm going. But I keep running. Fast. Faster . . .

I take a flying leap. *SPLASH!* I dive right into the giant water bowl.

Slurp. Slurp. Slurp.

Hey! This doesn't taste like water. It's too sweet. And too sour.

But it's cool and wet. And it stops my mouth from burning.

AAAAHHHH! My mouth starts to smile. It feels better.

But the two-legs aren't smiling. They look angry. And wet. Some of the sweet-and-sour water splashed on them.

The two-legs are yelling now. They're stomping their paws.

Those are some strange-looking paws. They have points on the ends.

I've never seen paws like that. Then again, I've never seen two-legs with upside-down food bowls on their heads, either. But that's what these two-legs are wearing.

"I'm sorry," I bark. "I couldn't see where I was going."

One of the pointy-pawed two-legs reaches out and grabs me.

Oh no. I know what can happen when a two-leg grabs you. They take

you to the pound! It happened to me once when my bone *kaboomed* me to London.

Wiggle, wiggle, jiggle, jiggle, whee! I slip out of his paws.

Thud! I land on the ground. That hurt!

"Sparky!" I hear Rex bark. "This way!"

I follow Rex through the crowd of people. I don't stop to pick up any more food. I just keep running.

Rex darts up some stairs. So I dart up some stairs.

He leaps up on a hard chair.

I leap up beside him. And then, suddenly, *the chair begins to move.*

It whirls. It twirls. It turns on its side.

SOMEBODY STOP THIS CRAZY
THING!

CHAPTER 4

Wiggle, waggle, whoa!

The chair has stopped spinning. But it feels like everything is still going around and around.

Rex leaps off the chair. He starts to walk away.

I start to follow Rex. *Wiggle, waggle, whoops!*

I fall down onto my belly.

My legs try to stand. But they're all wobbly.

Wiggle, waggle, whoops . . . again. I fall back down onto my belly. Now everything around me is spinning. My stomach is swishing and swashing and . . .

Uh-oh! *BLEHHHH!* All the food that was inside me is now *outside* me.

Two-legs leap out of the way. Some cover their noses with their paws.

I don't blame them. That food smelled a lot better going in than it did flying out. But I feel better now. Slowly, I stand up. My legs don't wobble. They work just fine.

My nose works just fine, too. It knows I stink.

Just then I spot some horses

drinking water from a giant wooden
bowl. That bowl is big enough to fit a
whole puppy. *Hmmm.* I don't usually
like baths. But . . .

Splash!

I jump into the big water bowl. I
wiggle to the right. I waggle to the
left. I wash that yuck right off of me.
NEIGH!

Uh-oh! Those horses don't sound happy.

"Hey, Rex!" I call as I leap out of the bowl and *shakity, shake, shake* the water from my fur. "Wait for me!"

"That moving chair was awful," I tell Rex as we walk around the rodeo a little while later.

"The Tilt-A-Whirl takes some getting used to," Rex agrees. "Sorry you got sick."

"Do you think there's more food at the midway?" I ask. "I want to put some of that barbecue back in my tummy."

"Sure," Rex says. "There's always food at the midway."

"You're so lucky to live at the rodeo," I tell him.

Rex gives me a funny look. "I don't live at the rodeo," he says. "It's just in town for a few weeks. After that I go back to searching for food on my own."

"Do you have a two-leg to live with?" I ask him.

Rex shakes his head. "I'm kind of a maverick. Been on my own ever since I can remember. It's fine while the rodeo's in town. But once the cowboys and four-legs go, it gets pretty lonely around these parts."

"What happens to the rodeo after it leaves here?"

Rex shrugs. "I guess the two-legs set it up in another town and do their rodeo jobs there, till they move on again."

"Jobs are really important," I say. "That's why I'm here."

"You want a job at the rodeo?" Rex asks.

I shake my head. "I need to learn a job I can do when I'm home. Otherwise Josh will get another dog. And I'll be a maverock, too."

"Mave*rick*," Rex corrects me. "But I don't see how having a job will keep your Josh from getting another dog."

"If I have a job, Josh will need me," I explain. "Like Samson's two-leg needs him to get his slippers."

Rex gives me a funny look. "I don't know what slippers are. Or who Samson is. But that's not a bad idea. I wonder if there's a job for me here at the rodeo. If I had a job, they'd have to take me with them when the rodeo moved on."

"Are there dogs at the rodeo?" I ask him.

"A few," Rex says. "Mostly there are cows, goats, sheep, and horses. But there's nothing they can do that a dog can't. I'm telling ya, Sparky, I'd be happier than a gopher in soft dirt if I could stay with the rodeo."

I'm about to ask Rex what that

means, when out of nowhere I hear a lot of two-legs shouting. Luckily, they don't sound mad. Just excited.

I turn around to see a mini two-leg riding on top of a shaggy four-leg. The four-leg is kicking his back paws in the air and wiggling his rear end.

"That there's the mutton-bustin' competition in the kiddy ring," Rex says. "Those sheep sure get mad when the mini two-legs try to ride 'em."

Baaaa, baaa, baaa.

That's a strange sound. I've never heard anything like it before. But it sure is loud.

BAM! Suddenly, a gate bursts open. A whole crowd of curly furred sheep bust their way into the ring.

"Uh-oh," Rex says. "That wasn't supposed to happen. It's supposed to only be one sheep and one two-leg at a time."

I guess nobody told the sheep that, because there are a whole lot of them in that ring.

AAAHHHHH! I hear the little two-leg shout. I think he's scared of all those sheep.

A group of two-legs leap into the ring. They're trying to catch the sheep.

BAAAAAA! The sheep are trying not to get caught.

Wiggle, waggle, wheeeeee!

Just then, I take a flying leap right over the fence. *Why did I do that?*

Now I'm running in circles, too. I'm trying to get those sheep to bunch together. *Wait, what am I doing?*

"Move, sheep!" I call.

The sheep all turn and stare at me.

Baaa, baaa! Some of them huddle together. I think they are scared of me.

A few sheep are still running around by themselves. I don't want them to do that. I want them to be near the other sheep.

I don't know why I want that. But I do.

I nip at the heels of one of the loose sheep. *Nip, nip, nip.*

Baaa! Baaa! He doesn't like that.

I nudge him with my nose. *Nudge, nudge, nudge.*

The sheep hurries over to his friends.

Another sheep follows after him. And another. And another. Now all the sheep are huddled together. *How did I know how to do that?*

THUD! Just then, the mini two-leg falls off the back of the sheep he was riding.

One of the big two-legs picks up the crying mini two-leg. He gives him a ride on his back as they leave the ring. That makes him feel better.

The sheep the mini two-leg was riding is running freely around the ring.

I need to get that one last sheep to join his friends.

"Move it!" I bark. I nip at his heels. I nudge him with my snout. "Go!"

And he goes.

Yes! That's right. I'm in charge of this ring!

Or maybe I'm not. There are two-legs running around the ring. Now they're chasing after *me*!

I can't let them catch me.

My paws run. Fast. Faster. *Fas*—

Uh-oh. I can't run any farther. The big herd of sheep is blocking my way.

"Move, sheep!" I bark. And the sheep start to move.

We all move through a gate. And then . . .

SLAM! The door shuts.

Baaa! Baaa!

The sheep sound mad. I don't think they like being stuck inside a cage.

And I don't like being stuck inside a cage with a bunch of angry sheep.

This is *baa-baa*-bad.

CHAPTER 5

"Help me, Rex!" I shout from inside the cage. "Get me out of here."

I'm not sure if Rex can hear me. After all, he's outside the cage, and I'm inside. And there's all this *baa, baa, baaing* going on.

"REX!" I shout again. "HELP!"

"Sparky, can you hear me?" Rex yells back.

"Yes!"

"I see cowboys over yonder," Rex tells me. "They're getting water for the sheep. When they bring the water in, you run out. *Just don't let 'em catch you.*"

Easy for him to say.

The cage door opens. One of the two-legs walks in. He's got an upside-down bowl on his head and a right-side-up bowl of water in his hands.

Now's my chance!

I put my head down and plow through the sea of curly furred sheep.

I slam into one sheep and push her to the side.

I scramble around another.

And I squeeze my way between two more.

Then, finally, I make my way out the door.

Wiggle, waggle, whee! I'm free!

A moment later, my buddy Rex is at my side. He has a big smile on his face. "You were amazing in that ring," he tells me. "Only a sheepdog could herd sheep like that."

"You heard the same sheep I heard," I say.

Rex laughs. "I meant that I've never seen anyone get sheep to move as a group the way you did. I don't know how the sheep all got loose like that. Those cowboys sure were lucky you were there to help get the sheep back in their pen."

I don't understand. I really didn't do anything. I just ran. And that made the sheep run. I didn't realize getting sheep to run was a job. Too bad we don't have any sheep at home.

Suddenly, my tongue pops out of my mouth. It just hangs there. Then my mouth starts panting.

"I think we oughta find you some water," Rex says to me. "You're lookin' mighty dry."

Rex leads me over

to a group of some of the strangest two-legs I've ever seen.

"There's always chow and cold water at the clown chuck wagon," Rex tells me. "Rodeo clowns know how to eat. Let's see if we can rustle up some scraps," Rex says.

These two-legs are wearing the same giant upside-down food bowls on their heads as the other two-legs I've seen here at the rodeo. And they've got the same pointy paws.

But these two-legs have very strange noses. They look like red balls in the middle of their faces. The kind of balls Josh and I use to play fetch.

Even stranger, these two-legs have big smiles on their faces. Usually, that wouldn't be strange. Two-legs smile just like dogs do. But these smiles are huge. And they don't move, even when the two-legs talk to one another.

Not *all* the two-legs are smiling. In the corner there's a two-leg whose smile is upside down. He has a water drop right under his eye.

The drop doesn't move. Not even when he blinks.

The smiling two-legs are all sitting together. They are eating and laughing. There are a few dogs sitting near them while they eat. I think they're waiting for some food to drop. But they aren't getting anything. These two-legs are neat eaters.

But the two-leg with the upside-down smile is by himself. I bet that's why his smile is upside down. I think that clown needs a friend.

We start sniffing around for food.

My tongue is still hanging out of my mouth. I'm really thirsty!

Just then, the two-leg with the upside-down smile walks over to Rex and me.

Uh-oh. Are we in trouble again?

The two-leg pulls out a tall, thin water bowl. He holds it up to my snout. My tongue reaches in and starts lapping up the cold water.

Aaahhhh! Lap, lap, lap.

The two-leg reaches over and pats me on the head. He pours more water into the tall thin bowl. And he puts it under Rex's snout.

Rex looks at him funny.

I think Rex is afraid. Maybe that's because Rex hasn't been friends with any two-legs.

Rex must be more thirsty than afraid, because he starts lapping up the water. The two-leg pets Rex on the head. His eyes seem happy, even though his smile is still upside down.

As soon as Rex finishes drinking, the two-leg begins to walk away. But before he does, he reaches down and pets Rex on the head one more time. I think he wishes he could stay with us a little longer.

"Where's he going?" I ask Rex.

"He's off to one of the rings, I reckon," Rex says. "That's where rodeo clowns do their jobs."

Jobs? That's just what we're looking for.

"What kind of job is he going to do?" I ask Rex.

"Clowns do many jobs at the rodeo," Rex explains. "There's only one way to find out what that clown's doing now. We're gonna have to follow him."

CHAPTER 6

We follow the sad-looking clown to the rodeo ring. But he doesn't look like he's working. He's just standing on the side of the ring, waving his upside-down food bowl in the air.

The clown isn't the only one in the ring, though. There's also a horse with a two-leg on his back. The horse is circling around some big round cans. They look kind of like the cans Josh dumps his food scraps into when he is finished eating.

I hate those cans. They get all the good food scraps.

"What kind of a job does that horse have?" I ask Rex.

"Barrel racing," Rex replies. "The horse has to run around barrels. He can't hit any of them or knock any over. And he has to do it really fast."

"That doesn't seem hard," I tell Rex. "We could do that."

"Rootin' tootin' right," Rex agrees. "And we could do it faster. Because anything a horse can do, a dog can do better. Wanna give it a try?"

"I sure do!" I cheer.

Barrel racing sounds like the perfect job for Rex and me. Rex could do it here at the rodeo with these big barrels, and I could do it at home with our little cans.

"Let's get in that ring and show 'em how it's done!" Rex shouts. He races for the ring and leaps over the fence. "Yeehaw!"

"Right behind you!" I leap over the fence, too. "Yeehaw!"

As soon as my paws hit the ground, they start running. I go around one barrel and then another.

Neigh!

The horse doesn't sound happy that Rex and I are in the ring. I think he's jealous. We run faster than he does. Especially Rex. His paws can really move!

"Come on, paws!" I yell. "Catch up to Rex!"

My paws move fast. Faster. *Fastest.* So fast that fur flies in my eyes. I can't see where I'm running.

SLAM! I run right into one of the big barrels.

But I keep running anyway. Fast. Faster . . . Ow! I did it again.

Neigh!

The horse is not happy. Neither am I. My head hurts.

I shake the fur away from my face so I can see. That's how I know that the clown with the smile that's upside down is running after Rex and me.

"Uh-oh," Rex says. "We better get out of here."

I follow Rex through a gate and out of the ring. The sad clown shuts the gate tight. Then he looks at Rex and me, and he laughs.

I've never seen anyone with an upside-down smile. Strange things sure happen at a Texas rodeo.

"Barrel racing wasn't as easy as it looks," I tell Rex. "The horse didn't have as much trouble barrel racing as we did. But he had help from that cowboy."

"You know, that gives me an idea," Rex says. "We don't need jobs of our own. We could just help the cowboys do *their* jobs. Make it easier on them."

I *thinkety, think, think* about that.

Samson helps his two-leg by getting his slippers.

And Frankie helps his by getting the paper.

Maybe that's what a dog's job is—helping his two-leg. Only . . .

"What could we help with?" I ask Rex.

"Well," Rex replies, "have you ever roped a calf?"

I cock my head. "I don't even know what that means."

"Come on, then," Rex says. "I'll show ya!"

72

CHAPTER 7

"There sure are a lot of events at a rodeo," I tell Rex as we walk over to another ring on the other side of the rodeo grounds.

"Yup," Rex says. "There are more than ten events every day. Calf roping is one of the best. And one of the hardest. Watch."

There, in the ring, a two-leg rides on the back of a horse. A minute later, a baby cow runs into the ring.

The two-leg on horseback swings something around and around in the

air. It looks kind of like
the leash that ties me
to Josh when we walk
in the park.

"What's he doing with that leash?"
I ask Rex.

"That what?" Rex asks. "Oh, you
mean the *lasso*. He's fixin' to throw it
around the calf's neck."

"Why doesn't he just get her a
collar and clip it on?" I wonder aloud.

"Get her a what?" Rex asks me.

Rex doesn't know what a collar or a leash is. He's never had a two-leg to walk beside in the park. That makes me sad.

The two-leg tosses one end of the leash toward the calf. But the calf runs away before it can go around her neck.

"That there's one feisty calf," Rex answers. "She's not going to make it easy."

"I didn't want to walk on a leash, either, at first," I tell Rex. "But it's kind of nice to know that Josh and I are tied together when we go for a walk."

The two-leg tosses the end of the rope again. The calf dodges out of the way.

"I'm gonna help that cowboy," Rex tells me.

"You're going to let him tie that leash—I mean lasso—around *your* neck?" That doesn't make sense to me. Walking on a leash doesn't sound like much of a job.

Rex laughs. "No. I'm gonna get that calf to stand still so the cowboy can just sling that lasso right over her head."

"You think you can do that?" I ask Rex.

"Sure as shootin'," he answers.

The next thing I know, Rex is in the ring, running toward that calf.

"Stand still, calf!" Rex barks. "Let the cowboy lasso you!"

But the cow doesn't speak dog. So

she keeps running. Only now she's trying to get away from the two-leg *and* Rex.

Rex charges toward the calf.

The calf dashes across the ring.

Rex zooms toward the calf.

The calf bolts away from Rex.

Suddenly the calf stops. Rex has her backed up against a wall.

"Hey, cowboy!" I hear Rex shout to the two-leg on the horse. "I got her cornered. Lasso her!"

But before the cowboy can ride his horse over to the cow, a group of funny-looking two-legs with balls for noses leap into the ring. They have smiles on their faces. But they have angry looks in their eyes.

I don't think the two-legs are there to tell Rex what a good job he's done. I think they're there to grab him!

"Run, Rex! Run!" I shout.

Rex looks back and sees the

clowns coming toward him. He takes
off running.

The clowns run after him.

The calf runs away from him.

The horse runs in circles.

There sure is a lot of running
going on in that ring.

And then, suddenly, Rex stops. He
has to. He's surrounded! Everywhere
he looks, there's a two-leg with a ball
on his nose.

One of them reaches out and picks up Rex. Oh no! What's that clown going to do with Rex?

"You have to get free!" I shout to Rex. "Jump! Jump now!"

But Rex doesn't jump. He just lies there, while the clown carries him out of the ring.

That's when I see the face of the clown. He doesn't have a smile on his face. He has a sad face. It's the clown with the smile that's upside down.

He's stroking Rex's back. He's trying to calm him down. And it's working. Rex isn't squirming. He isn't trying to get away.

The clown seems nice. But I don't know. This could be a trick. That dogcatcher in London tricked me with a bone before he threw me into the back of his metal machine and took me to the pound.

The clown carries Rex through a big gate. I sneak through before the gate can shut me out. I don't know where that clown is taking Rex. But I'm not letting him go alone. He's my friend!

The clown puts Rex down. He pets him on the head and walks away.

"Why didn't you try to jump out of his paws?" I ask Rex.

Rex shrugs. "I kinda liked the way it felt when he petted my back. I just knew he wasn't going to hurt me."

Rex is right. The sad clown didn't hurt him. He just brought Rex out here—to some place where there are a lot of metal machines with big round paws.

"What in tarnation?" Rex says. "How can these trucks be back already?"

"What's wrong?" I ask.

"When the trucks show up here in the parking lot, it means they're gonna pack up the rodeo and move on soon," Rex tells me. "You and I don't have much time to get this job thing figured out. I don't want them to leave without me . . . again."

"And I don't want Josh to get another dog," I say.

"Then we better get back into the rodeo," Rex says.

"But the sad clown threw us out," I remind him.

"We're not gonna let a little thing like that stop us!" Rex says. "We

gotta find jobs quicker than a hiccup.
Time's running out."

Rex is right. Time is running out.
For both of us.

86

CHAPTER 8

"I still don't understand what rodeo clowns do," I tell Rex as we walk back to the rodeo fairground.

"They help out with the events," Rex says. "And they make people laugh."

"I make Josh laugh a lot," I tell Rex. "Is that a real job?"

"Being a rodeo clown is more than just making people laugh," Rex says. "It's tough. Especially when it comes to bull riding."

"What's that?" I ask him.

"It's another event," Rex says. "Probably the toughest of the whole rodeo. A cowboy has to climb on top of a big bull and hang on for as long as he can. It's not easy, because the bull is kicking and bucking all the time. And bulls are strong."

I give him a funny look. "Why would a cowboy want to do that?"

"It's his job," Rex says.

"But what do the clowns do?" I ask. "They're not the ones sitting on top of the bull."

"Actually, the clown's job is a lot more dangerous than the cowboy's," Rex tells me.

"How?"

"I can't explain it," Rex says. "You have to see it to believe it."

YAHOOOOOOOO!

As Rex and I get near the ring, I hear a loud, frightening noise. My ears flatten against my head. My tail hides between my legs.

"Wh-what is that?" I ask Rex nervously.

"The two-legs," Rex tells me. "They're cheering at the bull-riding event."

"That's too loud to be two-leg cheering," I tell him.

"There's an awful lot of them in those bleachers," Rex points out. "Bull riding's the most popular event. Everyone comes to watch."

I look out into the ring. There's

a cowboy sitting on the back of a big angry bull.

"That bull is kicking hard," Rex says. "But the cowboy is holding on!"

YAHOO!

"Are the two-legs cheering for the cowboy or the bull?" I ask Rex.

"The cowboy," Rex says. "Why would they cheer for the bull?"

"Because he's standing up for himself," I explain. "He's trying to show the cowboy that this isn't his job."

"I never looked at it that way before," Rex admits.

GASP!

There's another loud noise. But this time it doesn't sound like cheering.

The cowboy flies off the bull and lands on the other side of the ring. He's lying on the ground. And the bull is charging right for him!

The cowboy gets up and starts to run away. The bull runs after him.

Suddenly another two-leg leaps into the ring. It's the sad clown. The one who gave us water. And who *didn't* take us to the pound. He's a nice clown. And now the bull is charging right for *him*!

"No, Sad Clown!" I bark. "Get out of there!"

But the sad clown keeps running around the ring. And the bull keeps running after him!

"I've got to help him!" I tell Rex.

One, two, three . . . *whee*! I leap over the fence and into the ring.

"Sparky, no!" Rex shouts as I leap. "The clown's okay. That's his job."

Rex may think the sad clown is okay. But I don't think so.

"Get out of the ring, Sad Clown!" I bark.

But the clown doesn't leave. Now we're both stuck here in the ring, with a very angry bull.

Grunt-grunt. Snort-snort.

And he's charging right for me!

94

CHAPTER 9

"Don't mess with Texas!"

I turn just in time to see Rex leaping into the ring. He's come to save me from the bull. Just like I came to save the sad clown.

Rex jumps up, higher than I've ever seen a dog jump. He lands right on the back of the bull. Wow! Rex is brave.

Grunt-grunt. Snort-snort. The bull is even madder now. It's not his job to give a dog a ride.

The bull kicks his hind legs high in the air.

"Hang on!" I shout to Rex.

"I'm trying!" Rex yells back. He wobbles a little on the back of the bull, but he stays put.

"Go, Rex!" I cheer.

YAHOOO! The crowd of two-legs cheers, too.

The bull kicks his back legs higher and harder.

"HEEEELLLLLPPPPPPP!" Rex shouts as he flies off the back of the bull.

Oh no! Any second now, Rex is going to crash on the ground. He could get hurt. It's going to be really . . .

All right. It's going to be really *all right*! The sad clown reaches out his arms. He catches Rex before he hits the ground!

The crowd of two-legs clap their paws together. They cheer. *YAHOO!*

Three more clowns rush into the ring. They force the bull into a cage.

Grunt. Snort.

That bull still sounds mad. But he can't hurt us now.

The clown with the sad face reaches into his pocket. He takes out a red ball and places it right on Rex's nose.

I wait for Rex to shake the ball off. But he doesn't. He just looks up and smiles.

The two-legs are cheering louder than ever. The sad clown has a happy look in his eyes, even though his smile is still upside down.

Rex's tail wags.

The sad clown reaches into his other pocket. He pulls out a long rope—I mean *lasso*—and ties it around Rex. He puts Rex down onto the ground. They start walking around the ring. *Together.*

Hooray! Rex has someone to be leashed to! And with that red ball on his nose, it looks like he has a job, too. He's a rodeo-clown dog!

Seeing Rex and his two-leg makes me miss *my* two-leg. It's time for me to leave the rodeo.

"Sparky, where are you going?" Rex calls to me.

"I have somewhere I gotta be," I tell Rex. "And you have a job to do."

"Sure as shootin' I do!" Rex cheers. "From now on, this clown and I are gonna be walkin' in tall cotton! Thanks to you."

"You're welcome," I tell him, although I'm not really sure what that means. All I know is that Rex is really, really happy.

Suddenly, I spy something on the ground. It's not food. But it's still pretty cool.

It's a bright red ball. I think it fell off one the clowns' noses.

I bet Josh and I could have a lot of fun playing fetch with that! I pick up the ball and head out of the rodeo. It's time to dig up my magic bone. It's time to go home.

CHAPTER 10

Diggety, dig, dig.

I'm back by the stinger-thinger bush. And I'm digging.

Diggety, dig, dig. Diggety . . . There it is! My magic bone. Right where I left it.

I can't wait to take a bite.

But I can't bite my bone while I've got this ball in my mouth.

I know. I'll wear the ball on my nose. Just like a rodeo clown!

I put the ball on the

ground and shove my nose into the hole in the middle of the ball. It feels a little funny. But it's just until I get home.

I look at my bone. I open my mouth and . . . *CHOMP!*

Wiggle, waggle, whew! I feel a little dizzy—like when I got off that chair that spun all around.

Stars are twinkling in front of my eyes, even though it's daytime! All around me I smell food—fried chicken, salmon, roast beef. But there isn't any food in sight.

Kaboom! Kaboom! Kaboom!

The *kabooming* stops, and I'm back in my own yard.

I race over to where the flowers are, and I start *diggety, dig, digging*. Dirt flies everywhere. This is one big hole!

I drop my bone in and push the dirt back over it. My bone is buried. No one can find it. Except for me, of course.

Just then, I hear a metal machine coming. It sounds like it's pulling up right outside my house.

Quickly I run through my doggie

door. I race through the house. I reach the front door just in time!

I sit on my back paws and wait. And then . . .

JOSH! JOSH! JOSH!

Josh opens the door. I jump up and lick him on the face.

Josh gives me a funny look.

"What's wrong, Josh?" I bark.

Josh pulls the red ball from my nose. He looks at it strangely. I guess he's wondering where the ball came from.

I wish I could tell Josh about Rex, the clowns, and the four-legs at the rodeo. Most of all, I wish I could tell Josh how I learned that I already have the most important job a dog could have.

But I don't speak two-leg. And Josh doesn't speak dog.

So instead, I go over to the chair where Josh left my leash this morning. I grab the leash between my teeth and bring it over to him.

Josh clips the leash onto my collar.

I smile at him. And Josh smiles back at me. He's happy because I'm doing my job.

It's my job to be Josh's friend. It's my job to make sure he's always got someone to be leashed to. And that he's never lonely.

I've got the best job in the whole wide world!

Fun Facts about Sparky's Adventures in Texas

Texas

The word Texas comes from the Hasinai tribe's word for friendship. That's the Texas state motto. Texas was the twenty-eighth state to join the United States, after declaring itself free from Mexican rule. Today, Texas is the second-largest state in the country. The only one that's bigger is Alaska. Texas is also the state with the second-largest number of people, right after California.

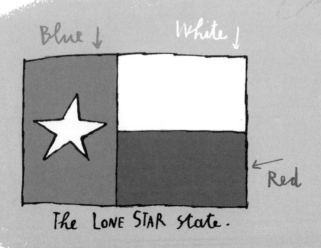

Blue ↓   White ↓

← Red

The LONE STAR state.

Rodeo

While rodeos now take place all over the country, the first rodeo is believed to have taken place in Pecos, Texas, in 1883. At that rodeo, cowboys competed in roping and riding events just like the ones you can see at rodeos today. Texas is home to the world's largest rodeo, the Houston Livestock Show and Rodeo, which takes place every March. That rodeo not only hosts cowboy contests, but also lets farmers show off their pigs, sheep, cattle, and other livestock. Like many rodeos, the Houston Livestock Show and Rodeo has a huge midway that features food, rides, and concerts by country-music singers and pop stars.

Cowboy Boots

No one knows who invented the pointy-toe shoes worn by cowboys and rodeo stars. Some people believe that boots that looked a lot like today's cowboy boots were worn by people in Southeast Asia more than 1,500 years ago. However, cowboys in Texas and other parts of the United States didn't start wearing their version until after the US Civil War, which ended in 1865.

The boots are made specially to help cowboys stay safe while they're riding horses. The pointy toe allows a cowboy to get his foot in the stirrup more easily. The heel keeps the boot from slipping out of the stirrup. The top part of the boot, which reaches just below the knee, keeps the cowboy's leg safe from snakes and thorny bushes.

Rodeo Clowns

Their painted faces might be funny, but being a rodeo clown is serious business. One of their many jobs is to protect a cowboy who has fallen during a bull-riding competition. The clowns distract the bull while the cowboy runs for safety. Then they help get the bull back into the pen.

About the Author

Nancy Krulik is the author of more than 200 books for children and young adults, including three *New York Times* Best Sellers. She is best known for being the author and creator of several successful book series for children, including Katie Kazoo, Switcheroo; How I Survived Middle School; and George Brown, Class Clown. Nancy lives in Manhattan with her husband, composer Daniel Burwasser, and her crazy beagle mix, Josie, who manages to drag her along on many exciting adventures without ever leaving Central Park.

About the Illustrator

You could fill a whole attic with Seb's drawings! His collection includes some very early pieces made when he was four—there is even a series of drawings he did at the movies in the dark! When he isn't doodling, he likes to make toys and sculptures, as well as bows and arrows for his two boys, Oscar and Leo, and their numerous friends. Seb is French and lives in England.

His website is www.sebastienbraun.com.